Dilly the BRAVEHEART

Story by **Dilly**

Written by **Penny Neer**

This is a work of fiction based on a true story.

First paperback edition June 2021

ISBN: 9798747334311 (Amazon) & 978-1-0879-0065-0 (Ingram Spark)

The author is grateful for permission to use the following material:

Page 8 (Adoption Ad) – Big Fluffy Dog Rescue   Page 9 (Stacked Dogs) – Andrea Doty

Page 11 (Dogs on Hind Legs) – Deb Chapman   Page 30 (Drum Major) – Isaiah Hole

Back Cover and Page 30 (Mace) – The Block M is a registered trademark of the University of Michigan, and is used with permission.

I wasn't always the "goodest" boy you see before you. No siree.

It happened like this . . .

— Dilly

Circle of Life   1

Winds of Change   2

Big Fluffy to the Rescue   6

Michigan Bound   12

This Smells Like Home   14

Neighbor Steve   16

Wrigley and the Zoomies   17

The Breakout   20

Yellow Day   21

Everywhere a Sign   24

Add Your Flavor   29

Goosies   32

Dilly the Braveheart   37

Map of Mud Lake   41

The Mud Lake Crew   42

Special Thanks   42

Connect With Dilly   43

Nuggets & Winks   44

Find 50 Things in the Map   45

Circle of Life

I knew every inch of the packed dirt circle I called home, the eight-foot chain a constant reminder I wasn't going anywhere. I didn't even have a name.

There weren't too many bugs in my matted fur because of its funky odor, like fumes rising from gasoline. When I caught a whiff of rain, I tried to collect a precious drink. Scraps people tossed my way were seldom within reach. A stray walnut was my only toy, and the shade of the doghouse was my sometimes friend.

Years ran together. Still, I wondered, *Would this be the day?* I just wanted to make a difference in a forever home, and to have a family that believed in me. If only I could see I might have a chance, but who would want a smelly old blind mutt? I didn't have much to offer, but things HAD to change.

And then one day, they did.

Winds of Change

With a rumble of thunder and the first hint of rain, I sought my rusty bucket. Sensing footsteps nearby, I sat up straight and gave a crooked smile. Maybe this human would toss me a morsel to munch or a wrapper to lick.

Suddenly, rough hands manhandled me into a crate. The scraping of wood on the metal bed of the pickup rattled my bones. My heart thunked against my rib cage.

Thrown about on the pitched road, I felt blood, warm and sticky, pasted on my nose. Smelly vapors followed like heat devils on hot pavement.

I had a feeling my life would never be the same.

I was dumped at a shelter, tethered and forgotten outside the back door. My ears flooded with the din of barking dogs, clanking doors, and shouts competing with the wind. While I couldn't see the gathering clouds, I could sense the darkness headed my way. It was a whirlwind as Hurricane Harvey aimed its course for Louisiana that last day of August.

3

I had weathered storms before and hoped this one would pass too. My wishes came true the next afternoon as an outfit called Big Fluffy Dog Rescue arrived to transfer the strays and misfits to safety in Tennessee.

Whimpers spilled from the filling van, but my croaking cry was not one of them.

My optimism dwindled as the crunch of their tires on gravel faded. Stranded like a castaway on the island of the shelter, the bitter taste of rejection lingered on my tongue.

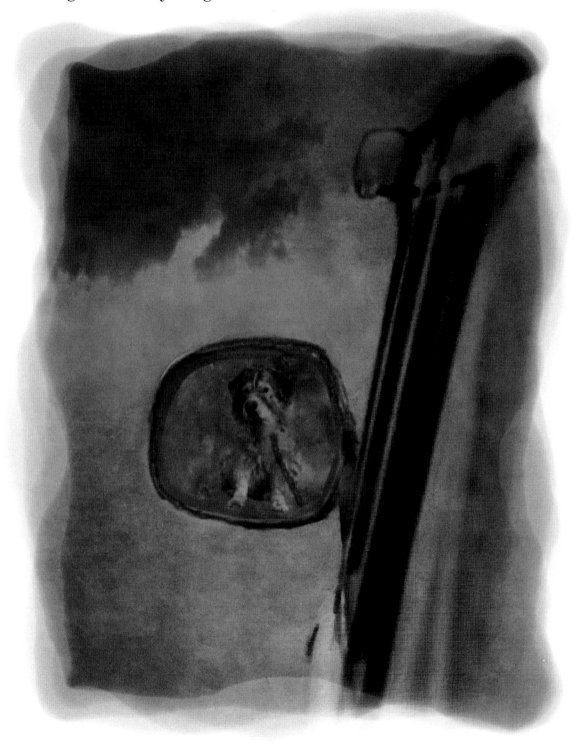

WHY? Why had I wished for things to change? How I longed for my old hut.

The shelter aide chased the departing vehicle, arms pin-wheeling. "Wait!" she shouted. "Is there room for one more?"

Is this a trick of the wind? Have they remembered this odiferous fur-ball after all?

My head lifted with my hopes as the BFDR team came back for this last gentle giant. It was a tight squeeze but I joined the knot of fuzz headed for Tennessee.

We rode through the night. With overworked senses and aching bones, I fell asleep to the rocking motion of the van.

6

Rolling to a stop at the BFDR facility in Nashville, passengers were unloaded and sorted by need. The knowledgeable squad deemed my matted coat to be beyond repair. Hands, understanding and gentle, shaved me. Years of loneliness drifted to the floor.

I had my first bath and heard the first kind words of my life. As the Big Fluffy Dog Rescue crew fussed over me, their compassion and care made me wonder—*Is this what love feels like?* Without the dingle-berries and hair looking like it had been coughed up by a cat, my life was already changed. 7

Eventually, my coat grew back and covered my leathery elbows. Still, no one adopted this Ewok-looking dog with sightless eyes. *Is the reason because, after years of neglect, I still don't know how to be a dog?*

A few weeks later I was assigned to a kind foster family. After many tears and goodbye hugs from the BFDR bunch, my journey continued.

At my new temporary home, the hubbub of other dogs greeted me. I felt like I was the scruffy different-looking guy, like a kid at a new school.

These other mutts misunderstood when I didn't return their invitations to play. All kinds of fluff-n-stuff went on in the yard. Others blamed me for stinky toots; they even made up mean names, calling them "barking spiders." An easy target, I tried to keep to myself.

There was one problem I didn't see coming.

9

Admiral, a sourpuss of a cat, was a trickster. He weaved willy-nilly through my legs so I tripped and he spilled my food for the others to gobble.

This pickle-puss sabotaged my path with his strategically placed hairballs. Vibes from Admiral's stink-eye scowls reached their mark.

Long days became long months.

One July morning, my ears perked at the familiar hum of the BFDR van. *Are they hauling me back?* Admiral's scheme to get rid of me must have worked. Dread sent sour saliva dripping from my mouth. I squeezed my ears shut, but muffled words trickled in—I would be heading north to Michigan. I tucked my tail in fear and it was as invisible as the unknown.

My foster-mates probably didn't even know or care that I was leaving.

Michigan Bound

After hours on the road, we reached Indiana. The door slid open and my crate unfastened. Fingers and fur braided as one and tears splashed my whiskers. A soft, soothing voice said that she was my new Mom and that my name was Dilly. Her hug swallowed me whole, melting a bit of my sorrow and fear.

My new Mom's sister, Aunt Lolly, nuzzled my muzzle. With treats called "scoobies" and the truck cleared of tools, the sisters lifted me into the back. At first, it was strange to not be in a cage and I couldn't pick a side. I even punched my snout up through the sun-roof.

I strained to push my head farther out the window and I felt like I was flying. From the cornfields and wildflowers to a farmer cleaning his barn, there were incredible smells! My nose could not look away. That is, until I accidentally stepped on the switch and rolled the window closed on my head.

12

"With my girls away at college, it's been pretty lonely," Mom said to Aunt Lolly. "I sure do miss them. Still, I've thought about this decision to adopt over and over again, like a tongue revisiting a lost tooth."

Aunt Lolly replied, "Well, you've sure had a lot of big fluffies through the years—three from the Humane Society and one from the ditch: Jake, Brindle, Fuzzy, and Bear. And we can't forget Teddy and Buster from when we were kids. You know what they say: 'The best way to honor the life of a pet you lost is to save another.'"

I didn't want to flub this fortune. I promised myself to do all I could to rescue Mom from ever being sad or lonely. My empty globes tried to thank her for taking a chance on me.

This Smells Like Home

Aunt Lolly's truck came to a stop.
  "Welcome to Mud Lake, Dilly!"
Mom said as she helped me out.
  My senses sprang to attention. I
thought, *This smells like home.*

Tentatively, I stretched my legs
after the long journey. I heard a
squirrel's scratchy claws as it ran
ribbons 'round a tree. A familiar
twang stained the air.
  *Could it be? There must be at least
ten walnuts. I am rich!*

14

I studied the festival of bird songs and scurrying critters. Lush grass carpet tickled my paws. Daylight faded and Mom said the sky wore a Michigan blue.

She asked, "Are you ready to meet Neighbor Steve tomorrow?"

I wondered, *What's a Neighbor Steve?*

The next morning Mom taught me to wait for the screen door to open before going outside. Five times she warned me, "Step!" as I maneuvered down from the deck.

I balked, not knowing what this Neighbor Steve character wanted with this old pooch. Yards past the walnut tree, a grizzled voice chuckled and offered a hand for me to sniff.

"We're going to be taste buds, Dilly," said Neighbor Steve.

I stood tall, my fluffy tail waving like a banner when he scratched behind my ears. Neighbor Steve let me lick the leftovers of lemon lush dessert. I couldn't remember tasting something so "Dilly-icious"!

My new buddy then produced real toys of every shape and texture. *Are these all for me?* What a change from the wrinkled walnuts I once knew. I chewed them gleefully with my nubby teeth. It was like Christmas in summer when Mom decorated a tree with his gifts. She didn't want to shred them with the lawnmower.

16

Wrigley and the Zoomies

Suddenly, a burst of energy swirled around me. *What is this commotion?*

"Looks like Wrigley has the 'zoomies'!" said Neighbor Steve.

Oh no, not again.

Aunt Lolly's dog, Wrigley, seemed wound up like a toy. From digging for clams in the lake to hopping from rock to rock, that little guy rarely stood still. He loved to chase the geese from the shore and could jump the seawall in a single bound.

Every sunup, he delivered a note strapped to his harness to Neighbor Steve. There was no limit to the pirate-pup's energy.

Wrigley's smile reached his stubby tail, even when treats were broken in half for us to share. He encouraged me, *Come on, Dilly Dawg. Shake your tail feathers, Big Guy!* Every day was a good day for that pupper with the superpowers.

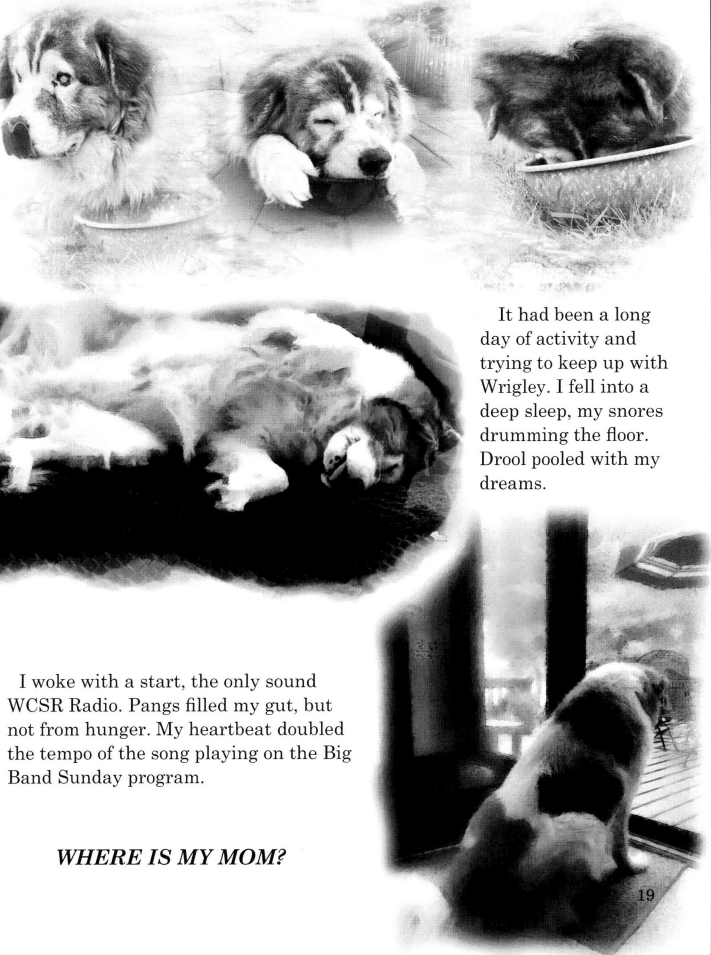

It had been a long day of activity and trying to keep up with Wrigley. I fell into a deep sleep, my snores drumming the floor. Drool pooled with my dreams.

I woke with a start, the only sound WCSR Radio. Pangs filled my gut, but not from hunger. My heartbeat doubled the tempo of the song playing on the Big Band Sunday program.

WHERE IS MY MOM?

19

The Breakout

I strained to hear any sign of Mom over Glenn Miller's Orchestra.

I had to find her!

After a moment's hesitation, I punched through the screen and counted the steps to the grass. I traveled in the only direction I knew—first came the toy tree, then by the squirrel buffet, and a few yards more to Neighbor Steve's house. I hoped he would know what to do.

My worries evaporated when we discovered that Mom had only gone to the mailbox. She chuckled when she saw me with Neighbor Steve and gave me a long hug as if she had been gone longer than just two minutes.

Wait till she spotted the screen door.

Yellow Day

The next morning Mom announced, "It's going to be a Yellow Day! We've got the maize of the sun to paint our path."

Mom piloted me through the grand park. We passed a picnic table where she and Aunt Lolly ate "ham-sammies" and reminisced about their Mom and Dad. The charred scar of the brush pile offered a waft of smoke. I detected a goldmine of critter caves in the seawall. Mom had cleared an opening in the rocks so I could maneuver to the lake for a drink.

At first it was exhilarating, but with each step, I grew more confused in the vast yard. Overwhelmed, I wondered how I would ever navigate so many obstacles. Hot tears threatened to spill. *Would Mom take me back to the shelter if she realizes I am blind?*

I needed a strategy. Maybe I could pretend to see by leaving tufts of my wool as clues. *Could a trail of fuzz help me find my way next time?*

I sprinkled my tumbleweed puffs the entire way so I could sniff out my route.

"Dilly, you're so generous to leave your fur for the birds to use in their nests. Good thinking!" Mom exclaimed. "They'll be comfy."

21

At sunrise, Mom woke me. "It's a day for doing. Let's not dilly-dally." She explained, "If you let your purpose be your alarm clock you'll pop up like toast. Then, spread your flavor on all you do." I liked the sound of that.

A carnival of scents floated like fairy dust. Today we would be dead-heading in the flower beds. That sounded scary and I didn't know what to do. *Would Mom send me inside?*

As she snipped the spent blossom heads, Mom told me that the flowers take turns blooming through the year and that the bees and moths team with the sun and rain to help them grow. Suddenly, a butterfly fluttered by, leaving a chalky trail of near-invisible sprinkles that tickled my nose. With Mom's laugh at my mighty sneeze, I swished my feather duster tail.

"Why Dilly, you're pollinating and reseeding the flowers too. We'll have colors for the rest of the summer."

With a fresh outlook, I searched for other opportunities to earn a treat from her pocket. I dug up weeds and held down the newspaper layers she covered with mulch.

I heard the unmistakable crinkle of a wrapper. "Here, I have a present for you. It's a backpack and a long leash so you aren't naked."

Wait—does Mom know my secret?

As if reading my thoughts, Mom found a way I could explore without straying off course.

What a relief!

Everywhere a Sign

One morning Mom and I strolled through the diamonds of dew and past the stone wall on our way to Aunt Lolly's cabin.

"I found a heart-shaped rock, Dilly! That's a sign of good luck. Signs are everywhere if we know how to discover them."

Near birch trees, I had a strange feeling I was being watched. Plopping flat like a pancake, I resisted their faint whispers. Mom thought trees could see in their own way, even though they don't have eyes.

Their stares made me wonder, *What do I look like? Are their leaves chuckling at this hound with the mask?*

Mom said I had a lightning bolt on my forehead, a lip curl Elvis would have loved, and a tail worthy of the cover of a romance novel. I resembled a lot of things, but not other dogs.

Self-conscious about my odd appearance, I hid my face.

"Dilly, you found nature's hairnet. You know, every web is unique. With a little mustache on your heart-shaped face, you're a one-of-a-kind too." Mom always knew what to say.

I have a lot to learn about "Dillyville." What a fantasy world of mysterious objects and wildlife here on Mud Lake!

I found magic around every corner.

It was an opportunity to face my fears and make some friends. My first attempt to hobnob did not go well. The opossum behaved rather stiffly and had no spunk at all.

One night, Mom said, "Even though it's a bright 'Dilly Moon' we still need a flashlight. We wouldn't want to step in something requiring the 'Super-Duper-Pooper-Scooper.'"

Just as I tried to make another new pal, Mom flew me around like a kite! *What is that awful smell?*

Add Your Flavor

The last of the dog days of summer slid into place. I learned to sense the emerald of cut grass, the ginger of crunchy leaves, the tangy citrus of crushed walnut skins—these were a few of the colors in my life's prism. My favorite hue was the yellow of a productive day.

With a new confidence, I yearned to leave my mark and make a difference. I reflected on possibilities to show my stuff.

I knew of Mom's pride in her daughters (my human sisters) because she talked about them all the time.
Do I have a special skill like they do?

McKenna was a drum major with the best band in the land. Mom always said to march to the beat of your own drum.

I already have a plume and I can strut, but the only thing I can twirl is my tongue.

My youngest sister Alana jumped so high when she played volleyball.
I can jump too, but I can't always find the ball.

I wished, *If only I could be like Aunt Lolly.* She was fantastic in racing her bike and using tools. Lolly always lent a helping hand. Unfortunately, these skills required thumbs.

Wrigley delivered his daily puppy-post to Neighbor Steve. *With my breath, could I send heartfelt misty signals?* But that only worked on cold mornings.

I sighed. *There has to be something I can do.* Nearby, Wrigley chased fish and snakes in the lake. His splashes gave me an idea. I trembled with anticipation as my plan came together.

I worried, *What if I don't do it right?*

My new spirit replied, *Oh, but what if I do!*

I turned away from Mom, and with my little nubs, prepared for action.   31

Goosies

I decided I would stop the geese long before they reached the shore. That way, we wouldn't need to watch where we stepped.

Wrigley isn't the only smart one on Mud Lake. Mom will be so proud of me!

After gnawing through my leash, I snuffled my way to the gap in the rocks. I waded into the squishy mud and slimy stones refreshed my paws.

Hundreds of geese lured me out with their taunting, *Honk at Dilly!* The symphony of squawks was music to my ears, convincing me to push for this mission.

The lake bottom disappeared beneath my mitts and my reflexes took over. My spirits were as buoyant as my fuzzy frame and I paddled freely without fear of bumping my "schnoz." Cool water swallowed any hesitation.

But, I soon doubted that I had inherited a natural ability to swim.

Have I bitten off too much?

My gut churned. I sputtered as my heavy coat became an anchor. I was in over my head in more ways than one. *What a bad decision I've made!* With slimy tentacles, panic seized my limbs.

I could no longer hear the mocking geese. My nostrils poked out like the blowholes of a baleen whale. The weight of my situation meshed with my saturated hide. Dreams of being rescued sank with my body.

Would I hug Neighbor Steve and Aunt Lolly ever again?
Hear little Wrigley's zoomies? Feel the wonder and color from
Mom's lessons?

I snorted one last time.

Magically, a hand grasped my mane, yanking me to the surface. Aunt Lolly swam and pushed the kayak while Mom dragged me alongside. It was slow going as Mom was unable to paddle one-handed and she struggled to avoid capsizing. Neighbor Steve tracked our progress through binoculars. To my rescuers, it must have felt like running during a nightmare.

Dilly the Braveheart

We finally collapsed safely onshore. *Is Mom upset with me? What would happen to me now?*

Mom's tears mixed with the lake water, her fingers laced in my soggy doggy fur. She told me I would learn to swim and the Mud Lake Crew would help me explore.

As the day came to a close, Mom said, "Oh, Dilly Dawg—You're so special and bring us such joy with your fuzzy ways and determination." Mom's forehead melded to mine. "You gave us a scare but you're still the 'goodest' boy."

I reflected on my journey and all I had learned. I belonged to a wonderful family, just as I had always longed for. I had amazing friends and could finally shed my worries. This time I was relieved to not be going anywhere— the chain that had once bound me had been replaced by love. A goofy grin filled my face.

This gentle giant with broken eyes had a vision.

I realized I could see all along.

I just needed to open my . . .

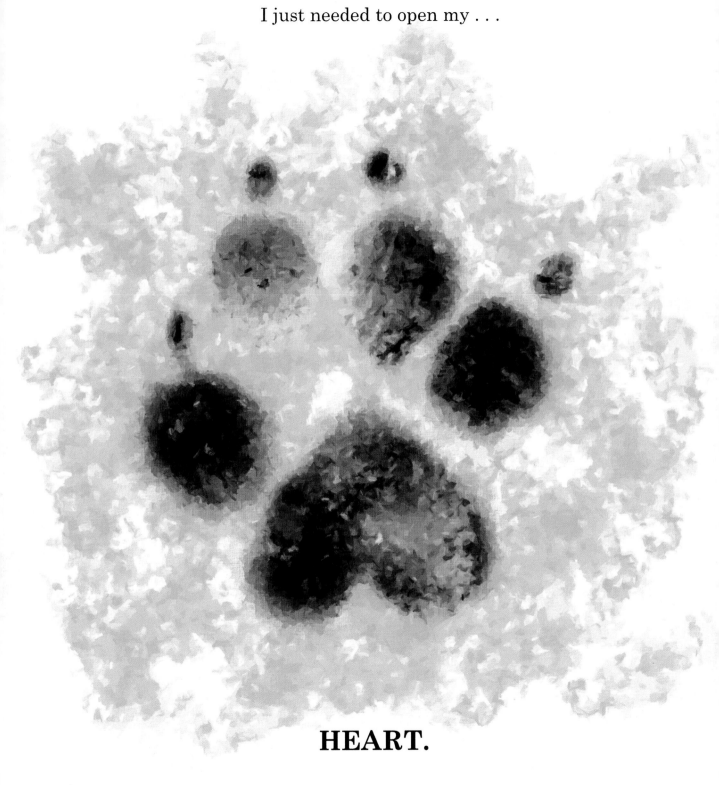

HEART.

40

Map of Mud Lake

Neighbor Steve's
Squirrel Buffet
Super Duper Pooper Scooper Area
Lolly's Landing
Big Fluffy Dog Rescue

RETURN and REST

41

The Mud Lake Crew

Dear Aunt Lolly, Wrigley, & Neighbor Steve,

We are forever grateful for the love and support you have given. Here's to you, the Mud Lake Crew!

Special Thanks

Dilly the Braveheart was a team effort. With the kindness and encouragement of family and friends, Dilly adds his voice to rescue animals and inspires us all. We would like to give special thanks for helping champion this book:

- Big Fluffy Dog Rescue – Jean Harrison (Executive Director), Sarah Lang Romeyn & Carrie Gandy (Transporters who drove through a hurricane, flooding and driving rain from Louisiana to Nashville), Nicole Butler (Coordinator), Foster Families, Tiffany Fintel & Kristi Bellomy (Drivers from TN to IN), and many tireless volunteers.

- McKenna and Alana, for your valuable feedback, glows, and grows.

- Donna English (Editing and Beta Reader) & Alex White (Beta Reader).

- Encouragement from members of Dilly's group & Cyndi Campbell Hoffman for the food.

- WCSR's Big Band Sunday (Andy Brown) and The Sauk Theatre (Trinity Bird & Gary Lee Minix).

The definition of "Dilly" is one who is remarkable, extraordinary, surprising, or unusual.

This true story of an abandoned dog with broken eyes reveals that Dilly is all of these things and more. There is so much more to his tale and all who have made it possible. For now, thank you and we do see you with our hearts.

— Dilly and Penny

Connect With Dilly

• If you enjoyed this book, kindly leave a review. Please tell us what it is about Dilly that stole your heart.

• Watch Dilly's 10 minute monologue online at https://www.YouTube.com/watch?v=r_EICHXmpiE

• See Dilly the Braveheart brand merchandise on Amazon. https://www.amazon.com/ s?k=Dilly+the+Braveheart&ref=nb_sb_noss_2

• There are many rescue animals in need. Please open your heart and adopt, foster, or donate. Big Fluffy Dog Rescue main site: **https://bigfluffydogs.com**

Nuggets & Winks

Cover – Dilly looks like a pansy flower and there is a heart on his face

Copyright page – A bluebird has Dilly's fur in its beak

Content page – Water dribbling is a hint that Dilly will have drool and a lake encounter

P1 – Barely visible walnut (his only toy – to the left of the pg #) and his rusty bucket

P2 – Vapors/fumes

P3 – Blood on Dilly's nose and yet another chain

P4 – Dilly is in the clouds as he is left behind

P5 – A chain is still binding Dilly; blood on his nose

P6 – Map of Southern US and the chain being left behind in Louisiana

P9 – Admiral the cat towering over Dilly foreshadows troubles

P11 – Admiral hidden on window sill wearing a smirk; Big Fluffy Dog Rescue Van

P13 – Rainbow coloring on Dilly's face & fur for dogs that have crossed the rainbow bridge.

P14 – "Objects are closer than they appear" hints that Dilly is closer to home than he knows

P15 – Music notes near robin

P18 – Turtle hidden on rocks

P21 – Bird with fur as Dilly leaves a trail and 2 heart-shaped rocks in sea wall

P23 – The newspaper being placed under the mulch is in German

P24 – Face in the birch when he feels he is being watched

P25 – Elvis lip curl

P27 – During daylight the opossum is playing "possum"

P28 – Night scene – Skunk, a D-shaped Dilly moon, a hidden face on the tree

P30 – M on McKenna's mace (for the Michigan Marching Band)

P31 – Dilly's breath is heart-shaped

P38 – The final scene is Dilly's actual paw print

Find 50 Things in the Map

1. Puddingstone
2. Cabin
3. Raccoon
4. Two turtles
5. Two squirrels
6. Coffee cup
7. Fur in a birdhouse
8. Spiderweb
9. Wasp nest
10. Swan
11. Snake
12. Toy Tree
13. 2 Muskrats
14. 2 Frogs
15. A robin
16. Gap in the seawall
17. Heron
18. Cardinal
19. 4 Chairs
20. 2 Butterflies
21. An old fisherman
22. Tulips
23. 5 Stone birdhouses
24. Picnic table
25. Goose
26. Aunt Lolly
27. Neighbor Steve
28. Mom
29. Wrigley
30. Road sign
31. October Glory maple tree
32. An arbor
33. One Inukshuk
34. Birch tree
35. Wood duck house

36. "Storage Shed"
37. Cat tails
38. Bridge
39. Gazebo
40. Lawnmower
41. Sprinkling can
42. 3 Pansies
43. Brush pile
44. 5 Heart-shaped rocks in the seawall
45. Waddles the Weather vane
46. Blue spruce pine tree
47. Kayak
48. Rock pile
49. 9 Dilly Dogs
50. "Return and Rest" bench

Made in the USA
Monee, IL
07 August 2024

63427217R00031